Falling in love . . .

Mr. Keen started to play the piano. I was busy watching Tina's feet. Every chance I got, I stomped on them as hard as I could.

I looked at her.

She was grinning.

"Doesn't that hurt?" I asked.

"No," Tina said calmly. "I'm wearing steel-toed shoes."

Wow. Tina was so cool. I'd never met a girl like her before.

Suddenly, I was aware of Tina's hand in mine. My heart started to beat harder. I knew exactly what was happening.

It was horrible.

It was awful. It was the worst thing possible.

I was falling in love.

Bantam Books in the SWEET VALLEY KIDS series

SWEET VALLEY KIDS

STEVEN'S BIG CRUSH

Written by
Molly Mia Stewart

Created by
FRANCINE PASCAL

Illustrated by
Ying-Hwa Hu

BANTAM BOOKS
NEW YORK · TORONTO · LONDON · SYDNEY · AUCKLAND

RL 2, 005-008

STEVEN'S BIG CRUSH

A Bantam Book / February 1996

*Sweet Valley High® and Sweet Valley Kids® are
registered trademarks of Francine Pascal*

Conceived by Francine Pascal

*Produced by Daniel Weiss Associates, Inc.
33 West 17th Street
New York, NY 10011*

Cover art by Susan Tang

ISBN: 0-553-48219-X

Published simultaneously in the United States and Canada

Bantam Books are published by Bantam Books, a division of Bantam
Doubleday Dell Publishing Group, Inc. Its trademark, consisting of the
words "Bantam Books" and the portrayal of a rooster, is Registered in the
U.S. Patent and Trademark Office and in other countries. Marca
Registrada. Bantam Books, 1540 Broadway, New York, New York 10036.

PRINTED IN THE UNITED STATES OF AMERICA

OPM   0 9 8 7 6 5 4 3 2 1

To Seanna Rachael Fallon

CHAPTER 1

Setting the Record Straight

Hi, I'm Steven Wakefield. That's right, Elizabeth and Jessica's big brother. I'm here because I want to set the record straight. I know you think my twin sisters are sweet and cute. Blond hair and blue eyes and all that. And you think they're special because they're twins, don't you? Ever since the twins were babies, people have been fussing over them. As if being identical were so special.

Being twins might be fun. But having twin sisters *isn't*. Sometimes

Jessica and Elizabeth dress up in identical outfits and try to fool Mom, Dad, and me. I never fall for their silly little tricks. After all, I'm two whole years older than they are. And much smarter.

I'm not a twin and I'm glad. In the whole world, there's only one Steven Wakefield. Nobody else has dark-brown hair and brown eyes like mine. Nobody else in the fourth grade at Sweet Valley Elementary School plays basketball as well as I do. My other big talent is eating. Once, on a bet, I ate four hot school lunches in a row. My best friend, Bob, didn't think I could do it. He had to pay me a dollar.

I ended up giving that dollar to Jessica so she wouldn't tell Mom and Dad that I—um, never mind. Just trust me: The twins are not all that

· sweet. You still don't believe me? OK, I'll prove it.

"Want to watch one of my greatest tricks?" I asked Bob. It was two weeks before Valentine's Day, and we were on the bus home from school.

Bob scratched his freckled face and shrugged.

"Are you telling me you don't want to see one of the greatest practical jokes ever?" I asked.

"I guess," Bob said. "Why? What are you going to do?"

"I already did it," I said. "Now we just have to wait for it to explode."

Bob was beginning to look interested. "Who did you play a joke on?"

"My sisters," I said. "See, I found a couple of Valentine's Day cards at home. I signed one 'Jessica' and one 'Elizabeth.' Then I put one in Charlie

3

Cashman's lunch box, and the other in Todd Wilkins's spelling book." Todd and Charlie are in the twins' second-grade class.

"This could be interesting . . ." Bob said.

"Very interesting," I said.

We settled back to watch. Our seat was in the rear of the bus, so we could see everyone. We didn't have to wait long.

About two minutes later, Charlie discovered his card. He waved it over his head. "Hey, you guys!" he hooted at the other boys. "Look at this!"

A second-grader named Jim Sturbridge was sitting next to Charlie. He looked at the card and laughed loudly. "Jessica sent Charlie a love letter!"

Elizabeth and Jessica were sitting just in front of the boys. They spun around. So did their friends Ellen

Riteman and Amy Sutton, who were sitting across the aisle.

"Jessica likes Charlie!" Jim sang out.

"I do not!" Jessica said.

Bob jabbed me with his elbow. "Here come the fireworks!" he said.

"May I please see that card?" Elizabeth asked Charlie.

"No," Charlie said.

"Give it to me!" Jessica shouted.

"Come and get it," Charlie told her.

Jessica snatched at the card, but Charlie held it out of her reach. "Stop it!" she yelled.

"Your face is red, Jessica," Ken Matthews called out.

"That's because she's in *love*," Jim said.

"I am not!" Jessica yelled. "I didn't write that."

"Did so!" Jim said. "And you signed it 'Hugs and Kisses'!"

Bob poked me in the ribs. "Nice touch."

"Thanks," I said.

"Ignore them," Ellen told Jessica.

Jessica's eyes were filled with tears. I felt a little bad for making her cry. She crossed her arms and stuck out her chin. "Dumb boys," she said. "Who cares what they say?"

The girls turned around in their seats and pretended not to hear anything.

The boys teased Jessica for a while longer. But when she didn't pay attention, they got bored and gave up.

"That was great," Bob said.

"The show isn't over yet," I said. "Don't forget about Todd."

Todd was sitting two seats up on the other side of the bus. He didn't notice his card until just before my stop. Then he read it quietly and put it away.

7

Bob yawned again. "Looks like that one is a dud," he said.

But I wasn't ready to give up hope. I spent the rest of the ride watching Todd. Nothing. What a letdown. I wanted to embarrass Elizabeth, too.

When the bus reached my stop, I punched Bob in the arm. "Later," I told him.

"See you," Bob said, and punched me back.

I slowly walked down the aisle and got off. Jessica and Elizabeth ran off the bus like they always do. What babies.

The twins were waiting for me on the sidewalk.

Elizabeth had her hands on her hips.

Jessica shook her puny finger in my face. "I know you sent that card, Steven!"

I shrugged. "So?"

"How could you be that mean?" Elizabeth asked.

"I'm your big brother," I told her. "I'm supposed to be mean to you."

"Well, you're going to be sorry," Elizabeth said.

"We're going to get you back!" Jessica said.

"Oooh, I'm shaking," I told them.

The twins stomped off toward home. I laughed at them.

Those two runts were no match for The Great Steven Wakefield.

CHAPTER 2

Mom's Nasty Surprise

"I want a window seat," Elizabeth said that evening as we were getting into the car. We were going out to dinner.

"Tough luck!" I pushed her out of the way and climbed into a window seat. "I got here first."

Elizabeth sighed and got in after me. Jessica followed her.

"Why do you always get the window seat?" Elizabeth asked me.

"Because I'm bigger than you," I said.

Elizabeth crossed her arms. "That's not a very good reason. If I were bigger than you, I'd share."

"Sure you would," I said, making a face.

"You can have my seat on the way home," Jessica said.

Elizabeth smiled at her. "Thanks."

Good. Let Jessica share. That way Mom and Dad wouldn't make me.

Mom and Dad got into the front seat. Dad started the car and pulled out of the driveway. Mom turned around to look at the three of us in the back.

"Steven, remember I said I signed you up for some lessons?" she asked.

"I remember," I said. Mom had told me a few nights ago that she had signed me up for some lessons, but she wouldn't tell me what they were—just that I'd have to wear a tie.

11

I was hoping she forgot. I hate ties.

"I signed you up for ballroom-dancing lessons," Mom announced.

"Ha, ha!" Jessica said immediately.

I frowned. I did *not* want to take dancing lessons. Even my stupid little sister was smart enough to know that.

"Dancing lessons?" I asked.

"Yes!" Mom said, sounding happy with herself.

"Mom, please," I said. "Don't make me do it!"

"What's the big deal?" Mom asked. "You'll have fun."

Elizabeth and Jessica traded happy looks. They love to see me miserable.

"Dad, please," I said. "I'm begging you! Dancing lessons are for nerds."

"Really?" Dad gave me a look in the rearview mirror. "I took dancing lessons when I was your age. Are you saying *I'm* a nerd?"

12

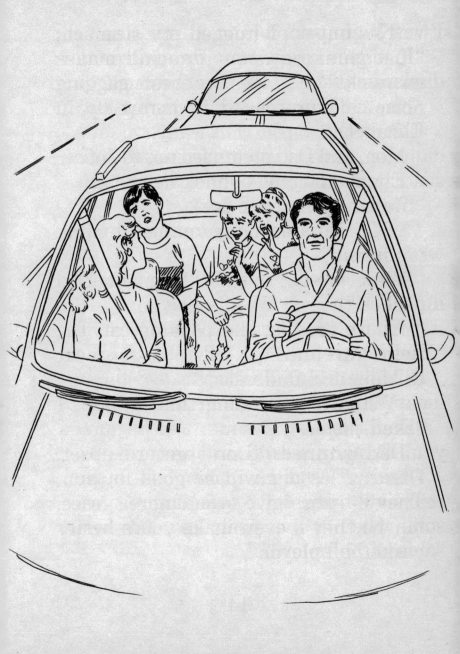

"No, but—" I hugged my stomach. "Just thinking about dancing makes me sick!" I made my best gagging noise and pretended to throw up in Elizabeth's lap.

Mom and Dad pretended not to notice.

Elizabeth calmly shook her head.

Jessica rolled her eyes.

OK, so it's an old joke. *I* still think it's funny.

When we got to the restaurant, Dad parked the car. We all piled out.

As we crossed the parking lot, the twins ran ahead. I fell into step next to Mom and Dad.

"Why are you doing this to me?" I asked them.

Dad grinned. "Don't get so upset. Dancing lessons will be good for you. They'll—um, give you more grace. Maybe they'll even make you a better basketball player."

"Besides," Mom added, "the school had a special offer this month. I paid cash. No refunds."

Once Mom said that, I knew I was sunk. My parents would never change their minds now.

"How often is this class?" I asked.

"Twice a week," Mom replied. "Tuesday and Thursday afternoons."

Jessica and Elizabeth were waiting for us at the door to The China Sun, which is our favorite Chinese restaurant.

"At least I won't have to spend those days with the creeps and their baby-sitter," I said. For the past few weeks, Mom had been working in the afternoon. A girl named Molly came over to watch the twins.

"She's *our* baby-sitter," Elizabeth said.

"Not mine," I said. "*I'm* not a baby."

Jessica stuck her tongue out at me.

"That's enough," Dad told us.

We walked into the restaurant.

"I'll take you shopping tomorrow," Mom said to me.

"Shopping?" I asked. I really hate to shop.

Mom nodded. "You have to wear nice clothes to the class, including a tie."

A *tie*? Talk about nerdy!

"Mom, please be reasonable," I said. "I don't want to take dance classes!"

"I don't want to hear any more about it," Mom said in a no-nonsense voice. "You're going. It'll be fun. Bob is in your class. I saw his father while I was signing you up."

At least *that* was good news. "What else do I have to wear?" I asked Mom while Dad talked to the hostess.

"Dress pants and a button-down shirt," Mom said.

I groaned.

"Mom, is Steven going to have to dance with girls?" Elizabeth asked.

"Of course," Mom said.

My heart sank. Girls? Yuck! Girls are gross. There was only one way to deal with this dance class: I was going to have to run away from home.

"This way, please," the hostess said.

I started to follow Mom and Dad to the table. Jessica and Elizabeth pushed by me. They were dancing like a couple in an old black-and-white movie.

"Steven, I love your tie," Jessica said as they spun in circles.

"Thank you!" Elizabeth made a kissy face.

"Steven, darling, you dance wonderfully," Jessica said.

I noticed people at other tables were watching them.

17

"Mom!" I yelled.

"That's enough, girls," Mom said. "Don't embarrass your brother."

Jessica and Elizabeth stopped dancing and started giggling wildly.

Mom was smiling.

So was Dad.

I was definitely running away! But not right then. I was too hungry. Maybe after dinner . . .

CHAPTER 3
Secret Plans

"I'm really bummed about this stupid dance class," I told Bob at school the next morning. We were trying to finish our math homework before class started. "I almost ran away from home last night."

"So why didn't you?" Bob asked.

I chewed on my pencil and thought about that.

"When we got home from dinner, I was too full," I said. "I ate all my food and most of the twins', too." Having little sisters does have a few benefits—

like getting to eat all their leftovers.

"Well, I'm glad you didn't run away," Bob said. "Dance class is going to be fun."

"Fun?" I asked. "Dancing with girls—fun?"

Bob nodded. "I thought of some great jokes we can play."

I smiled slowly.

Bob was the biggest girl-hater in the world. I was second biggest. Together, we had played tons of jokes on the girls in our class. But then our teacher had decided to "keep a better eye on us." She moved our seats to the first row, right in front of her desk. That ended our fun. But dance class was a whole new opportunity. The teacher there didn't know we were troublemakers. Yet.

I copied another problem out of my math book.

Bob glanced up at me. "Class starts tomorrow," he said, looking thoughtful. "I know exactly what I want you to wear—"

"We have to wear dress pants and a tie," I said with a groan. "My mom's taking me shopping this afternoon."

"We'll wear that junk, and something else. . . ." Bob leaned closer, so that none of the other kids would hear. He whispered his secret plan in my ear.

When he told me what that *something else* was, I started to cheer up. I still didn't want to learn ballroom dancing. But maybe—just *maybe*—the class wouldn't be completely awful.

CHAPTER 4

The Purple-Toe Squad

The next afternoon, I slowly walked into a big room at the dance school. A sign taped on the door read BEGINNING BALLROOM. I could think of a thousand places I would have rather been. Like the principal's office at school.

A bunch of girls were standing together near the windows. Most of them weren't from my school.

On the far side of the room was a group of boys—including Bob. I hurried over to them.

Bob was looking at a bulletin board on the wall. It showed photographs of kids dancing. They all looked miserable.

"Hi," I said.

"Hi," Bob said. "Did you wear your hiking boots?"

I held up one of my big, heavy boots. "Yup!"

Bob and I exchanged high fives.

"Say hello to the Purple-Toe Squad," I said.

"We're going to stomp those girls' toes until they're mush," Bob said.

"Pulp!"

"Soup!"

"One dance and they'll be maimed for life," I said.

"All right!" Bob yelled.

"Shh," I said. "Here comes the teacher."

Quickly, I took my new tie out of my

pants pocket. I hadn't wanted to put it on until the last moment. I tied it as best I could.

The teacher stood in the middle of the room and beamed at us. He was skinny, and his thin white hair stood up in fluffy tufts.

"I'm Mr. Keen," the teacher boomed. "Are you all ready to dance?"

"I am!" called out a neatly dressed boy with curly brown hair, freckles, and wire-rim glasses. The rest of us snickered at him.

"What a loser," Bob whispered to me.

I nodded.

But Mr. Keen looked delighted. "What's your name?" he asked the boy.

"Tom." He didn't look even a little bit embarrassed.

"OK, Tom," Mr. Keen said. "You're going to dance with this young lady

24

here." He took the hand of a very tall girl with wavy blond hair and pulled her forward. "What's your name?"

"Sally," she whispered.

"Tom, meet Sally," Mr. Keen said.

Sally smiled uncomfortably.

Tom grinned like a geek.

Mr. Keen paired kids up until we all had partners. Mine was named Tina.

"Hi," she said.

I rolled my eyes at her. I might have to *dance* with her, but nobody could make me *talk* to her.

Mr. Keen started to show us how to do some dumb dance called a waltz. Bob and I didn't pay much attention. We were making faces at each other across the room.

After a few minutes, Mr. Keen hurried over to the piano.

"Positions!" he yelled.

Tina looked at me.

I didn't move.

Tina sighed heavily. "You're supposed to put one hand on my waist like this." She grabbed my right hand and put it in place. "I put my hand on your back. Now hold my other hand."

I couldn't believe it. Who thinks this stuff up? Talk about torture!

Mr. Keen started to play the piano. "*One,* two, three. *One,* two, three," he called out.

The other kids began to move around the room.

I was busy watching Tina's feet. Every chance I got, I stomped on them as hard as I could.

"Stop it!" Bob's partner, Lucy, screamed from across the room. "Ouch! You hurt me!"

Mr. Keen jumped up and ran over to Bob and Lucy. "What's the matter here?"

"He was jumping all over my feet!" Lucy yelled.

Bob grinned.

Mr. Keen frowned at him. "You two can sit down until Bob here learns to behave," he said.

Bob and Lucy sat down. Mr. Keen considered *that* punishment? I was jealous of them.

Mr. Keen went back to the piano and started to play. I went back to stomping on Tina's feet. Only harder this time.

Nothing.

I looked up at her.

She was grinning.

"Doesn't that hurt?" I asked.

"No," Tina said calmly. "I'm wearing steel-toed shoes."

My jaw dropped. "How did you know to do that?"

Tina laughed. "We take dance in

28

gym at my school. Only there, it's me and my friends who stomp on the *boys'* feet."

Wow. Tina was so cool. I'd never met a girl like her before.

I looked at her more closely. She had light-brown hair and bright-green eyes. She wasn't *too* ugly.

Suddenly, I was aware of Tina's hand in mine. My heart started to beat harder. I knew exactly what was happening.

It was horrible.

It was awful. It was the worst thing possible.

I was falling in love.

CHAPTER 5

Smiley Faces Are Not Cute

"Steven!" Dad called up the stairs. "Hurry up. Breakfast is ready!"

I opened my eyes and shook myself awake. Breakfast was ready? Why hadn't someone woken me up earlier? I sat up quickly. Usually, I get washed and dressed before I eat. But I'd do that later. Breakfast was ready and I was starving.

As I climbed out of bed, I noticed my face felt funny. Itchy. But I didn't pay attention. I ran downstairs as fast as I could. I didn't want my breakfast to get cold.

"Morning," I mumbled, rushing into the kitchen.

Dad looked up from his newspaper. When he saw me, he spit his coffee out all over his bowl of oatmeal.

Mom turned away from the counter. "Ned, what's wrong—" She didn't finish her sentence, because once she saw me, she burst out laughing.

The twins were sitting at the table. They were giggling like little monkeys.

"What's so funny?" I demanded.

Nobody answered. They were all too busy laughing at me.

I ran into the guest bathroom and looked in the mirror. When I saw myself, I almost fainted. There was all kinds of makeup junk on my face. I looked like a girl!

The twins must have sneaked into my room while I was sleeping. . . .

Jessica walked by the bathroom. "Got you, Steven."

Elizabeth was right behind her. "Got you good!"

I closed my eyes so I wouldn't have to see my reflection for another horrible painful second. The twins had got me back for my valentine trick. They thought they were so funny. I was not amused.

But I wasn't going to let them ruin my day. It was Tuesday. That meant I'd get to see Tina. I'd spent the whole weekend thinking about her.

"You're late," Bob whispered to me when I rushed into dance class that afternoon. "I was scared you weren't coming."

"It's not my fault," I grumbled.

Thanks to the twins, I'd been running late all day. Scrubbing that makeup junk off my face had taken so long, I'd missed the bus. Then I was late to school. I'd never caught up.

I spotted Tina. She was standing near the windows, talking to Sally. My palms started to sweat.

Mr. Keen came into the room. When he saw me, his smile faded. "Steven," he said sternly, "where is your tie?"

"Right here, sir!" I pulled my tie out of my pocket and stared at it in horror. My nice normal navy-blue tie was gone. Instead, I was holding a bright-green tie covered with bright-yellow smiley faces. Someone had given it to Dad for Christmas last year. As a joke. The twins had pulled a switch on me somehow.

Everyone in class was watching me. My cheeks were burning. My sweet

little sisters had already got even that morning. When were they going to leave me alone?

Mr. Keen was waiting. I had no choice. I took a deep breath and put the tie on. Everyone laughed when they saw it.

"Very original!" Mr. Keen winked at me.

Please just let me disappear, I thought. I counted to three, but nothing happened.

"Now that Steven is ready, we can dance," Mr. Keen said. "Let's start by working on the waltz some more."

Great, now I have to dance the whole class wearing this stupid tie, I thought. *I hope Tina will still speak to me.* I wanted to be able to dance with her again.

"You may keep your partners from last time," Mr. Keen told us.

All right! *Maybe Mr. Keen isn't such a bad guy, after all,* I thought. My heart was thudding as I walked toward Tina.

She made a face at me. "I can't believe I'm stuck with you again," she said.

"I wish I'd worn my hiking boots," I said.

"That trick is so old!" Tina rolled her eyes.

Mr. Keen started to play. "*One,* two, three."

I put my arm around Tina and we began to dance. Or tried to dance, anyway. I was in heaven.

"Bob," Mr. Keen said sharply. "You'd better behave. I'm watching you."

When Mr. Keen turned around, Bob stuck his tongue out at him.

I slowly sneaked my hand up and pulled lightly on Tina's hair.

"Steven!" Tina said with a giggle. "What are you doing?"

"Don't pay any attention to me," I said. "You need to think about your dancing. I know dogs who dance better than you."

"And I know monkeys who dress better than you." Tina looked at my tie.

I felt a tiny shiver of happiness run up my back. Tina liked me, too! I could tell from the way she was acting.

"Bob, I saw you poke Lucy," Mr. Keen called out. "I think she's put up with you long enough. I want you two to switch partners with Tom and Sally."

Sally did not look pleased.

Bob was already the most hated boy in dance class. I was envious. But I knew I had to be good. I didn't want Mr. Keen to make *me* change partners. I didn't want to dance with anyone but Tina.

CHAPTER 6
Twin Enemies

"Don't be long at the video store," Mom called from the front porch that evening. "The pizza will be here soon."

"We'll hurry," Dad called back. "Come on, kids. Hurry it up."

Jessica, Elizabeth, and I climbed into the car. Since Mom wasn't with us, there were enough window seats to go around. But I got the front seat.

"How was dance class today?" Jessica asked after Dad started to drive toward the mall.

"It was all right," I said.

"How were the *girls*?" Elizabeth asked.

I immediately thought of Tina. "Fine," I mumbled.

"Steven's turning red," Jessica said in a singsong voice. "Steven's turning red!"

"I am not!" I yelled.

"Yes, you are," Elizabeth said. "Do you like any girls in your dance class?"

"Did they like your tie?" Jessica said.

The twins started to giggle.

"For your information, she liked it a lot," I said.

"She?" said Jessica.

"She?" said Elizabeth.

"Leave Steven alone," said Dad.

Dad pulled into the video-store parking lot at the mall.

"Steven likes a girl!" Jessica said.

"No, I don't," I said. I didn't want

them to find out anything more. I rushed past them into the store.

"This won't take long," I told Dad, changing the subject. "We already know what we want to rent."

Dad and Mom had said the twins and I could pick out a video. I was excited. A creepy werewolf movie had just come out. I was dying to see it. And I knew the twins were, too.

"What do you want to get?" Dad asked. He held the door open for the rest of us.

"Full Moon," I told him.

"Is that OK with you girls?" Dad asked.

Elizabeth and Jessica traded looks.

Jessica bit back a smile. "No! We want a movie about . . ." I just *knew* she was trying to think of something I'd hate.

"Ballerinas!" Elizabeth supplied.

"How about *The Red Shoes*?" Dad asked. "That's a classic."

"OK," Jessica and Elizabeth said together.

"No!" I yelled. "I don't want to see some dumb girls' movie."

Dad glanced at his watch. "Well, let's vote."

"Red Shoes," Jessica said immediately.

"Red Shoes," Elizabeth agreed.

"Full Moon," I said sadly.

"Sorry, Steven." Dad stepped up to the counter. "It's two against one. Now, let's get some help and get out of here."

"But, Dad!" I yelled. "Of course it was two against one. Elizabeth and Jessica are *twins*. They never disagree."

"Steven, please," Dad said. "I'm not in the mood for an argument."

Jessica stuck her tongue out at me.

Boy, was I mad! Especially since I knew the twins wanted to see *Full Moon* as much as I did. They'd just got that dumb ballerina movie to be mean.

Dad quickly checked out the movie. Soon we were back in the car. I got the front seat again.

"Know what?" Jessica asked Elizabeth.

"What?"

"I think Steven likes a girl," Jessica said.

I twisted around in my seat and gave her a look.

Elizabeth smiled at me sweetly. "I wonder who she is."

"I don't know," Jessica said. "But I'm going to find out."

My stomach dropped down to my toes. Not that I'm scared of a couple of seven-year-olds. But Jessica could be pretty sneaky when she tried. I definitely didn't want her to find out about Tina.

Dad pulled into our driveway. The pizza delivery truck was parked in front of our house.

"The pizza's here!" Elizabeth yelled.

"Perfect timing," Dad said.

The rest of them jumped out of the car. They rushed toward the house. I followed slowly. I wasn't excited at all about the movie. And I'd lost my appetite for pizza. Having twin enemies in my own family was not fun.

CHAPTER 7
Tina Gets Weird

Something was wrong.

At dance class on Thursday, Tina didn't put me down. Or hit me. Even though we were trying to dance the fox-trot together, she was pretending I didn't exist.

Things got so boring, I gave her hair a good yank.

Tina jumped away from me. "Cut that out!"

I was surprised. Tina had giggled when I'd pulled her hair before. Why was she mad now?

"Is there a problem, Tina?" Mr. Keen asked in a tired voice.

"Yes!" she replied. "Steven pulled my hair. I don't want to dance with him anymore. I want to dance with Tom."

"Fine," Mr. Keen said.

From across the room, Bob gave me a thumbs-up.

But I was heartbroken. Why was Tina doing this? Didn't she like me anymore?

Tina marched over to Tom. His latest partner, a redhead named Eva, came over to me. She did not look thrilled.

Mr. Keen began to play again.

While Eva and I danced, I watched Tina and Tom out of the corner of my eye. They were laughing. *Tina and I used to laugh like that,* I thought sadly.

I wasn't surprised Tina had picked Tom as her new partner. He was all of the girls' favorite. He never stepped on their toes—not even by mistake. In fact, he was the best dancer in the whole class. I hadn't cared until Tina wanted to dance with him.

For the rest of class, I kept hoping Tina would ask to be my partner again. She didn't. When class was over, she left without saying good-bye to me.

"The way you pulled Tina's hair was great," Bob said as he gathered up his stuff.

"Yeah," I muttered. While I waited for Bob, my eyes drifted to the photos on the bulletin board. I saw something that made my heart jump.

"What's this?" I was staring at a photograph someone had pinned up. It was of me and my cousin Robin. The caption read "Steven Wakefield and his girlfriend." I recognized Elizabeth's handwriting.

Bob looked over my shoulder. "Hey, who's that? I didn't know you had a girlfriend."

"I don't!" I yelled. "That's my cousin!"

"Sorry," Bob said.

I angrily ripped the photograph off the bulletin board. "The twins did this. I don't know how. But they're going to pay!"

"What's the big deal?" Bob was looking at me as if I were crazy.

"What if Tina saw this?" I asked.

Bob narrowed his eyes. "Do you like Tina?"

If I had told Bob the truth, he would have died from the shock.

"No way," I said.

Bob broke into a grin. "I'm glad. I'm planning a major gross-out for the girls," he added in a low voice.

"Good luck," I said darkly as we walked out of the room. "Mr. Keen spends half his time watching you. You're going to have a hard time pulling anything off."

Bob put his arm around my shoulders. "That's where you come in, Wakefield. I want *you* to play the joke."

"Oh." Even though I was talking to Bob, I was thinking about Tina. Had she seen the photograph? Is that why she had been so unfriendly during class? Maybe I could tell her I didn't really have a girlfriend. . . . No. That would be almost like telling her I liked her. Impossible. Especially for a chicken like me.

"Will you do it?" Bob asked.

I sighed. "Sure. What do I have to lose?"

After all, I'd already lost Tina.

CHAPTER 8
Talk Radio

Right after dinner that night, I locked myself in my room. I love my room. It's the only place I can get away from the twins.

I flopped down onto my bed and tried to figure out what was up with Tina. Was it possible to make her like me again? I was willing to do anything. . . . But what should I do? I needed advice. But I couldn't ask Mom. Or Dad. Or any of my friends.

A snack will help me think, I told myself. I went down to the kitchen.

Mom was sitting at the table. She was doing homework for a class she takes on interior design.

"Hi, honey," Mom said.

"Hi," I said. "Do we have any cookies?"

"In the closet," Mom said. "Just don't eat too many."

"OK," I agreed.

The radio was on in the kitchen. I listened to it while I searched for the cookies.

"This is *Desperate and Dateless*, the show that answers your questions about love," the announcer said. "Do we have a caller?"

"Yes, hello?" came a woman's high-pitched voice.

"Go ahead, caller," the announcer said.

"How can I get my husband to help with the dishes?" the woman asked.

I spotted a bag of oatmeal-raisin cookies and pulled it out. "Mom, what are you listening to?"

"Hmm?" Mom looked up at me. "Oh, I'm not really listening to that. Jessica turned it on."

"Oh," I said.

I put the bag back and started toward the door with a handful of cookies.

"Use a plate," Mom said.

I sighed and went back for a plate.

As I was climbing the stairs, I had an idea. I could call *Desperate and Dateless* for some advice!

I ran back into my room, turned on my radio, and found the right station. When the announcer gave out the station's phone number, I copied it down. Then I tiptoed out into the hallway, picked up the phone, and dialed. It was busy. I had to try six times before I got through.

"KSVR," a man said after the phone had rung many times.

"Hi," I said. "I have a question for *Desperate and Dateless*."

"Please hold," the man said.

I waited for five minutes more before someone else finally picked up. "Go ahead, caller." It was the announcer!

"Am I on the radio?" I was starting to get nervous.

"Yes," the announcer said. "How old are you?"

Oh, no! *Desperate and Dateless* probably didn't take calls from kids.

"I'm old enough to have a problem with love," I said in my best deep voice.

The announcer laughed. "What's your name?" he asked.

"S-Smiley," I said, looking at the smiley-face tie on my bed.

"OK, Smiley. What's your problem?"

"I like this girl," I said. "And I thought she liked me, too. But now she's acting strange. She won't even talk to me."

"Hmm," the announcer said. "Have you told her how you feel?"

"Well—no," I admitted.

"Then that's what you have to do," the announcer said. "Tell her you love her. Honesty is always the best policy."

"But—" I started.

"Thank you for calling," the announcer said quickly. The line went dead.

As I hung up the phone, my stomach flipped over. I didn't like the advice I had just got. There was no way I was going to tell Tina I *loved* her.

But maybe I could tell her I *liked* her. It wouldn't be easy. . . . But I had to do it! If I didn't, Tina might become

Tom's girlfriend instead of mine.

I walked down the hall toward my room. Suddenly my heart started to pound.

Jessica and Elizabeth were standing in their doorway with big, dumb smiles on their faces.

How long had they been spying on me?

"Hi, Smiley," Elizabeth said.

Oh no! I thought miserably. "What? Who's that?" I asked.

"You were calling *Desperate and Dateless!*" Jessica said. "We heard you on our radio."

"I was not!" I yelled. "I—I don't even know what you're talking about."

"Do so, Smiley!" Elizabeth said. They both started laughing.

I ran down the hall and into my room. I slammed my door. *Why weren't you more careful?* I asked myself. The twins had just got their first radio. They loved it. I should have guessed they'd be listening.

Well, it wasn't my fault I couldn't think straight! The twins were driving me crazy! And if they found out I had a girlfriend, they'd never leave me alone.

The sad thing was I *didn't* have a girlfriend. All I had was a crush. But I was going to do something about that. . . .

CHAPTER 9

Steven, the Chicken

About an hour later, I sneaked out of my room. I waited till it was almost my bedtime, so Jessica and Elizabeth would be asleep. I tiptoed downstairs to the den.

Mom and Dad have a desk there where they keep lots of important things. Like letters from our teachers. And the dance-school phone list.

My hands were shaking as I pulled out the blue paper and found Tina's phone number. I'd never called a girl on the phone before. It was scary.

Brrring.

My heart was beating so loudly, I could hardly hear the phone ring.

Brrring.

"Hello?" It was a girl's voice. And it sounded just like Tina! I suddenly realized I had no idea what I was going to say. Could I just blurt out "I like you" and then hang up?

"Hello?" the voice said again.

"Hi. Is Tina there?" I managed to say.

"Sure. Just a minute."

I waited, listening to the blood pound in my ears.

Just then Jessica ran into the den. She was in her pajamas, but she was still very much awake.

"Who are you calling *now*?" Jessica asked. "*Desperate and Dateless* has been over for an hour."

"Get lost," I said.

Jessica instantly became glued to the spot. She put her hands on her hips and waited. *Why couldn't I have been an only child?* I thought unhappily.

"Hello?" Tina said over the phone.

I couldn't tell Tina I liked her while Jessica was listening. I didn't want my bratty little sister to hear. I didn't want *anyone* to hear. I wasn't sure if I could even say the words out loud.

Quickly, I hung up.

"What's the matter?" Jessica asked. "Wasn't your girlfriend home?"

I pushed by her without answering. Maybe if I ignored her, she'd disappear.

Up in my room, I noticed the box of valentines I'd used to send messages to Todd and Charlie. It was still sitting on my desk. Seeing the valentines gave me an idea. I could write

Tina a valentine and give it to her on Valentine's Day.

First I put a chair in front of my bedroom door. Then I carefully chose the right valentine. I wrote my message and signed it. Then I hid it someplace the twins would never dare to look: in my dirty-clothes basket.

CHAPTER 10

Bob Gets in the Way

On Valentine's Day, on the bus home from school, I started to feel sick to my stomach. The idea of giving the valentine to Tina terrified me. And I'd planned to do it at dance class that afternoon. In other words, *soon*.

I did have one thing to be happy about. Elizabeth had gone over to Amy's house to play. I had only one twin to avoid.

At home, I went right to my room. With sweaty fingers, I took Tina's valentine out of its hiding place.

"Steven!"

Jessica's voice surprised me so much, I dropped the card.

"What?" I snapped.

Jessica was standing in my doorway. She was grinning an evil little grin. "There's a *girl* on the phone for you."

"Really?" I said in a voice that sounded high and squeaky.

Jessica nodded. "Maybe it's your girlfriend."

Oh, wow! Jessica was right. It had to be Tina! But why was she calling me?

My legs felt weak as I walked to the phone in the hallway. Jessica was watching me. I couldn't talk to Tina with the brat around. So I ran downstairs to the den. Before Jessica could get in, I closed the door and locked it. At last, some privacy.

I picked up the phone and willed

myself to sound cool. "Hello?"

Someone on the other end of the line giggled. And then there was a sound like someone picking up another phone.

"Tina?" I said.

Another giggle.

"One, two, three," someone whispered.

"Steven's got a girlfriend," three voices said together. "Steven's got a girlfriend, Steven's got a girlfriend!"

My face heated up. I recognized Elizabeth's, Amy's, and Jessica's voices. Jessica must have picked up the phone in the hallway upstairs.

Shaking with anger, I banged down the phone. On top of being angry, I was sad. I'd been really happy when I'd thought the call was from Tina.

I started up the stairs to get Tina's card. About halfway up, I changed my mind again. Maybe the valentine *wasn't* such a good idea. What if Tina showed it to her friends? What if Bob saw it? Maybe it would be better just to *tell* Tina I liked her. That way she wouldn't have any proof I'd said it. If anyone asked, it would be her word against mine.

The card was still in my bedroom when I left the house.

I'll tell her as soon as I get to class, I decided as I hurried toward the dance school.

When I walked in the door, I spotted Tina right away. She and Sally were listening to Tom play the piano. The girls both looked impressed. I really didn't like that guy at all.

I took a deep breath and marched toward Tina.

"Steven!" Bob rushed up to me.

"Not now," I said.

"Now," Bob said, grabbing my arm. "Class is about to start. I have to tell you what to do."

"What to do about what?" I asked, turning to face him.

"About my joke, what else?" Bob asked.

"You want to play it *today*?" I'd been so busy thinking about Tina that I'd forgotten all about Bob's joke.

"Yeah," Bob said, pulling me over to the side of the room. "I have everything you'll need."

"Listen, Bob, I don't know—" I started.

But Bob was already fishing through his book bag. "OK, here's the plan." He leaned close and started to whisper in my ear.

When I heard what he had in mind—and who I was supposed to play the joke on—I wanted to tell Bob to get lost. But I chickened out. Again.

CHAPTER 11

The Joke's on Me

"Today we'll practice the fox-trot again," Mr. Keen said a few minutes later. "Grab your partners, kids!"

My heart was beating double time. *Please don't let Tina dance with me,* I thought.

Eva had been my partner in the last class. But she was whispering with Tina about something. When the girls finished whispering, Eva joined hands with Tom. Tina walked toward me, smiling shyly.

A few minutes earlier, I would have been thrilled. Now I was severely bummed out.

"Happy Valentine's Day," Tina whispered to me as we started to dance.

"Er—thanks." I glanced down at my pocket, almost hoping the bottle Bob had given me had disappeared. Unfortunately, it hadn't.

Bob was watching me from across the room. After a few minutes, when I didn't do anything but dance, he steered his partner my way.

"Go on," he whispered as they foxtrotted by.

I closed my eyes and took a deep breath. At the same time, I slipped my hand out of Tina's and put it in my pocket.

"Is something wrong?" Tina asked.

"Yes!" I said loudly. "I think you have a nosebleed!"

Tina stepped away from me. "No, I don't—"

Before she could say anything more, I squirted the fake blood Bob had given me all over her dress. Some of it got on my hands, too.

"Yuck," I said loudly. "You bled all over!"

Mr. Keen had stopped playing. The room had got very quiet.

Tina was glaring at me.

Sally stepped toward Tina. "Are you all right?"

"Of course!" Tina said angrily. "This is just another one of Steven's stupid jokes."

Bob started to laugh. So did the rest of the boys, except that creep, Tom. Most of the girls were laughing, too.

For a second, I felt proud.

But then Tina stomped her foot. "I

hate you, Steven Wakefield!" she yelled. Then she ran out of the room.

"Tina, wait!" I called after her. "I'm sorry!"

"Leave me alone!" Tina yelled.

"Tina!" Mr. Keen jumped up and ran after her. He gave me an angry look as he left the room.

Bob came up to me. "That was great," he said, patting me on the back.

"Shut up!" I told him.

Bob took a step back. "What's wrong with you?"

"Tina is never going to talk to me again," I said. "And it's all your fault!"

"Why do you care?" Bob asked.

"I just do, that's all," I said.

"You like her, don't you?" Bob asked.

I was staring at my shoes. "Maybe," I whispered.

Bob started laughing.

"What's so funny?" I snapped.

"It's just that I thought you hated girls," Bob said. "I thought you thought guys who liked girls were losers." I realized Bob looked sort of embarrassed.

My jaw dropped. "*You* like girls?"

Bob nodded.

"Then why are you always playing jokes on them?" I asked.

"To get their attention," Bob said.

I sighed. Thanks to Bob, I'd got Tina's attention, all right. But not the kind of attention I wanted.

Tom came up to us, shaking his head. "You really blew it," he told me.

"What do you mean?" I asked.

"Everyone knows you like Tina," Tom said. "And she's never going to talk to you again."

What a disgusting little know-it-all!

"Yes, she will," I said.

"I don't think so," Tom said.

"Just you watch!" I told him.

Bob gave me a high five. "Go for it, buddy," he said.

CHAPTER 12

I'm No Quitter

I ran out into the hallway. Mr. Keen was on his way back in. "Where do you think you're going, young man?" he asked. He did not sound friendly.

"Did you find Tina?" I asked.

"No," Mr. Keen said.

"Well, I'm going to," I said.

"Steven, come back here right now!" Mr. Keen shouted.

But I was already out the door. I paused on the sidewalk for a second, breathing hard. Tina was nowhere to be seen. I was scared Mr. Keen was going to come out and drag me back inside. That's when I remembered the dance-class phone list. It had addresses for all of Mr. Keen's students. Tina had probably gone home. I could go to her house and tell her I was sorry.

Maybe I'd even tell her I liked her.

I started to run toward home to get the phone list.

Thinking about telling Tina I liked her made me feel like throwing up. I changed my mind back *again*. A written message would be better. I'd get the valentine from my room and give Tina that.

At home, I quietly sneaked in the door. I could hear the twins talking to Molly in the kitchen. Making as little noise as possible, I dashed up the stairs. I got the valentine and hurried out into the hallway.

A blond, blue-eyed monster was waiting. Elizabeth.

"What are you doing home?" she asked.

"Nothing," I said, inching backward. Someone standing behind me snatched Tina's valentine out of my hand. I spun around. It was Jessica. I should have known she'd be nearby. I had fallen right into the twin monsters' trap.

Jessica started to open Tina's card.

"Don't!" I yelled. "That's personal!"

"Dear Tina . . ." Jessica read in a sickly sweet voice.

"Is that valentine for your girlfriend?" Elizabeth asked.

"No!" I yelled.

"Is so," Jessica said. "Listen to the rest of this: *I think you're very pretty. I like you. Happy Valentine's Day. Steven.*"

Elizabeth was giggling like crazy.

I'd had it! "I'm never talking to another twin for as long as I live," I growled. Then I grabbed the card out of Jessica's hand and marched down the stairs. Jessica and Elizabeth were still laughing. I tried not to pay attention.

"Where are you going?" Jessica called after me.

I didn't answer.

"Can we come?" Elizabeth asked.

I opened the door and walked outside.

Jessica and Elizabeth were right behind me.

"We're coming, too," Jessica said.

"We want to meet your girlfriend," Elizabeth added.

Where was Molly? Why didn't she notice when Jessica and Elizabeth ran after me?

"I bet Tina is ugly," Jessica said as the twins hurried down the street behind me.

"We'll find out soon," Elizabeth said.

"I wish we had a camera," Jessica said. "That way we could show a picture of Steven's girlfriend to all our friends."

I winced. Didn't I tell you having twin sisters was no fun?

CHAPTER 13

Tina's Secret

"Do you think he's going to kiss her?" Jessica asked Elizabeth as they trailed me down the sidewalk.

"I hope not," Elizabeth said.

"If they kiss, I'm not watching," Jessica said.

"Me, neither," Elizabeth said.

The twins had nothing to worry about. There was no way I was going to kiss Tina. But I didn't tell them that.

I found the right house number. Just thinking about being at Tina's made me dizzy. Especially considering that the twin monsters were right behind me. I put my hand on her gate and took a deep breath. Then I opened the gate and started down the path. I had Tina's valentine clutched in one hand.

The twins skipped after me.

"Go away," I shouted, but they didn't listen.

I climbed the steps to Tina's porch, swallowed hard, and rang the doorbell. As soon as I did, I wanted to run away.

But there was no time. The door swung open almost immediately. Tina stood staring at me.

The twins fell silent when they saw her. I almost wished they would say something—so I wouldn't have to.

"May I help you?" Tina asked.

My heart ached. Tina was acting

like she didn't even know me! She must have been really mad. . . .

"Tina, I'm sorry about what happened at dance class," I said in a rush.

"But—" Tina said.

I held up one hand to silence her. I knew if I didn't say what I had to say fast, I'd chicken out again.

"Also, I made you this valentine." I thrust the card into Tina's hand.

"Thanks, but—" Tina said.

"*And,*" I interrupted, "I, well, it's just—I like you!"

"But I'm not Tina!" the girl burst out. "I've been trying to tell you: I'm Gina, Tina's twin sister. Tina's not home right now."

My jaw dropped. Tina had never mentioned she had a twin sister!

Gina burst out laughing. "You just gave a valentine to someone you've never met before!"

Jessica and Elizabeth were laughing, too.

"Steven's girlfriend is a twin!" Elizabeth exclaimed. She and Jessica jumped up and down.

I couldn't take any more. I dashed down the path faster than the twins could follow. *I'm going to hate girls forever,* I told myself. *Especially twin girls.*

When I got home, Molly was sitting on our front steps. She looked worried.

"Have you seen the twins?" she asked me.

"Yeah," I said. "They're right behind me."

Molly let out all of her breath. "That's good!"

"No, it's not," I muttered. I started to push past Molly. But she held out a red envelope.

"Someone stopped by and left this

for you," Molly said. "She said she was a friend from dance class."

"*She?*" I squeaked out.

Molly nodded. "You'd better hide that before the twins get back."

She was right. I grabbed the card. Then I ran inside and upstairs to my room. I locked the door and leaned against it. With shaking fingers, I opened the letter. It was a valentine from Tina.

Dear Steven, it read. *Even though you act stupid sometimes, I still like you. Happy Valentine's Day. Tina.*

I closed the card with a happy sigh. Tina liked me! That surprising news turned my miserable day into the happiest Valentine's Day in my whole life. Maybe *all* twins aren't so bad.

But twin *sisters* are the worst.

I was in my room, admiring Tina's valentine, when I heard two pairs of footsteps coming up the stairs. It could only mean one thing. The twins.

"Steven," Jessica yelled, "come out of your bedroom,"

Oh great, now they want to tease me about Tina some more, I thought. I ignored them.

"Steven," Elizabeth said, "open the door. We need to talk to you."

"No way," I said. If they wanted to bug me some more, they could forget it.

Then the two pests started knocking on the door. I put a pillow over my ears, but they knocked harder and harder. "Please open up, Steven," they shouted.

Finally I couldn't take it anymore. I opened the door. "OK, what do you two twerps want?" I asked.

"We're going to have a family meeting to talk about our vacation," Elizabeth said. The twins smiled sweetly.

"That's what you wanted?" I asked. "You didn't want to bug me, or tease me, or play a cruel joke?"

"No. We're going to have a vote to decide where we want to go," Jessica said.

Another vote! I didn't like the way votes usually went in our family—I remembered how Jessica and Elizabeth had won the videotape vote last week. *But maybe this will take their minds off Tina for a while,* I thought as my sisters and I bounded downstairs.

Where will the Wakefields pick to go on vacation? Find out in Sweet Valley Kids #66, AND THE WINNER IS . . . JESSICA WAKEFIELD!

SIGN UP FOR THE SWEET VALLEY HIGH® FAN CLUB!

Hey, girls! Get all the gossip on Sweet Valley High's® most popular teenagers when you join our fantastic Fan Club! As a member, you'll get all of this really cool stuff:

- Membership Card with your own personal Fan Club ID number
- A Sweet Valley High® Secret Treasure Box
- Sweet Valley High® Stationery
- Official Fan Club Pencil (for secret note writing!)
- Three Bookmarks
- A "Members Only" Door Hanger
- Two Skeins of J. & P. Coats® Embroidery Floss with flower barrette instruction leaflet
- Two editions of *The Oracle* newsletter
- Plus exclusive Sweet Valley High® product offers, special savings, contests, and much more!

Be the first to find out what Jessica & Elizabeth Wakefield are up to by joining the Sweet Valley High® Fan Club for the one-year membership fee of only $6.25 each for U.S. residents, $8.25 for Canadian residents (U.S. currency). Includes shipping & handling.

Send a check or money order (do not send cash) made payable to "Sweet Valley High® Fan Club" along with this form to:

SWEET VALLEY HIGH® FAN CLUB, BOX 3919-B, SCHAUMBURG, IL 60168-3919

NAME_____
(Please print clearly)

ADDRESS_____

CITY_____ STATE_____ ZIP_____
(Required)

AGE_____ BIRTHDAY_____ /_____ /_____

SWEET VALLEY KIDS

Jessica and Elizabeth have had lots of adventures in *Sweet Valley High* and *Sweet Valley Twins*...now read about the twins at age seven! You'll love all the fun that comes with being seven—birthday parties, playing dress-up, class projects, putting on puppet shows and plays, losing a tooth, setting up lemonade stands, caring for animals and much more! It's all part of SWEET VALLEY KIDS. Read them all!

☐	JESSICA AND THE SPELLING-BEE SURPRISE #21	15917-8	$2.99
☐	SWEET VALLEY SLUMBER PARTY #22	15934-8	$2.99
☐	LILA'S HAUNTED HOUSE PARTY # 23	15919-4	$2.99
☐	COUSIN KELLY'S FAMILY SECRET # 24	15920-8	$2.99
☐	LEFT-OUT ELIZABETH # 25	15921-6	$2.99
☐	JESSICA'S SNOBBY CLUB # 26	15922-4	$2.99
☐	THE SWEET VALLEY CLEANUP TEAM # 27	15923-2	$2.99
☐	ELIZABETH MEETS HER HERO #28	15924-0	$2.99
☐	ANDY AND THE ALIEN # 29	15925-9	$2.99
☐	JESSICA'S UNBURIED TREASURE # 30	15926-7	$2.99
☐	ELIZABETH AND JESSICA RUN AWAY # 31	48004-9	$2.99
☐	LEFT BACK! #32	48005-7	$2.99
☐	CAROLINE'S HALLOWEEN SPELL # 33	48006-5	$2.99
☐	THE BEST THANKSGIVING EVER # 34	48007-3	$2.99
☐	ELIZABETH'S BROKEN ARM # 35	48009-X	$2.99
☐	ELIZABETH'S VIDEO FEVER # 36	48010-3	$2.99
☐	THE BIG RACE # 37	48011-1	$2.99
☐	GOODBYE, EVA? # 38	48012-X	$2.99
☐	ELLEN IS HOME ALONE # 39	48013-8	$2.99
☐	ROBIN IN THE MIDDLE #40	48014-6	$2.99
☐	THE MISSING TEA SET # 41	48015-4	$2.99
☐	JESSICA'S MONSTER NIGHTMARE # 42	48008-1	$2.99
☐	JESSICA GETS SPOOKED # 43	48094-4	$2.99
☐	THE TWINS BIG POW-WOW # 44	48098-7	$2.99
☐	ELIZABETH'S PIANO LESSONS # 45	48102-9	$2.99

A BANTAM SKYLARK BOOK

FRANCINE PASCAL'S

SWEET VALLEY

Twins AND FRIENDS.®

- ☐ **BEST FRIENDS #1** .... 15655-1/$3.25
- ☐ **TEACHER'S PET #2** .... 15656-X/$3.25
- ☐ **THE HAUNTED HOUSE #3** .... 15657-8/$3.25
- ☐ **CHOOSING SIDES #4** .... 15658-6/$3.25
- ☐ **SNEAKING OUT #5** .... 15659-4/$3.25
- ☐ **THE NEW GIRL #6** .... 15660-8/$3.25
- ☐ **THREE'S A CROWD #7** .... 15661-6/$3.25
- ☐ **FIRST PLACE #8** .... 15662-4/$3.25
- ☐ **AGAINST THE RULES #9** .... 15676-4/$3.25
- ☐ **ONE OF THE GANG #10** .... 15677-2/$3.25
- ☐ **BURIED TREASURE #11** .... 15692-6/$3.25
- ☐ **KEEPING SECRETS #12** .... 15702-7/$3.25
- ☐ **STRETCHING THE TRUTH #13** .... 15654-3/$3.25
- ☐ **TUG OF WAR #14** .... 15663-2/$3.25
- ☐ **THE OLDER BOY #15** .... 15664-0/$3.25
- ☐ **SECOND BEST #16** .... 15665-9/$3.25
- ☐ **BOYS AGAINST GIRLS #17** .... 15666-7/$3.25
- ☐ **CENTER OF ATTENTION #18** .... 15668-3/$3.25
- ☐ **THE BULLY #19** .... 15667-5/$3.25
- ☐ **PLAYING HOOKY #20** .... 15606-3/$3.25
- ☐ **LEFT BEHIND #21** .... 15609-8/$3.25
- ☐ **OUT OF PLACE #22** .... 15628-4/$3.25
- ☐ **CLAIM TO FAME #23** .... 15624-1/$2.75
- ☐ **JUMPING TO CONCLUSIONS #24** .... 15635-7/$2.75
- ☐ **STANDING OUT #25** .... 15653-5/$3.25
- ☐ **TAKING CHARGE #26** .... 15669-1/$3.25

Buy them at your local bookstore or use this handy page for ordering:

Bantam Books, Dept. SVT3, 2451 S. Wolf Road, Des Plaines, IL 60018

Please send me the items I have checked above. I am enclosing $_____
(please add $2.50 to cover postage and handling). Send check or money
order, no cash or C.O.D.s please.

Mr/Ms _____

Address _____

City/State _____ Zip _____

SVT3-1/94

Please allow four to six weeks for delivery.
Prices and availability subject to change without notice.